THE CAVES

LIZARD

BENJAMIN HULME-CROSS

Illustrated by
Nelson Evergreen

A & C BLACK
AN IMPRINT OF BLOOMSBURY
LONDON   NEW DELHI   NEW YORK   SYDNEY

First published 2014 by A & C Black,
an imprint of Bloomsbury Publishing Plc
50 Bedford Square
London WC1B 3DP
Bloomsbury is a registered trademark of Bloomsbury Publishing Plc

www.bloomsbury.com

ISBN 978-1-4729-0106-4

A CIP catalogue for this book is available from the British Library.

Printed and bound in India by Replika Press Pvt Ltd

1 3 5 7 9 10 8 6 4 2

The Teens can choose prison for life … or they can go on a game show called The Caves.

If the Teens beat the robot monsters, they go free. If they lose, they die.

I am Zak. Sometimes I help the Teens. Sometimes I don't.

The Teens were called Carl and Mel. They looked scared. They ran to the caves.

The Voice spoke.
"The game begins in 10 minutes."

I went into the caves after the Teens.
They didn't see me.

The Teens were shouting.

"I didn't steal it!" Carl said to Mel.

"You stole it!" said Carl. "Why didn't you tell them that you did it?"

"Why should I?" said Mel.

I looked at Carl. I thought he was telling the truth.

I took an axe and a knife out of my bag. I put
them on the ground.

Then I crept back outside.

There was a cage on the rocks. Inside the cage, there was a lizard.

It had long, sharp teeth and it was huge.

The cage door opened.

The lizard ran into the caves to find Carl and Mel.

I ran behind the lizard.

I could hear the Teens shouting.

The lizard was getting closer to them.

I knew a faster way through the caves. I ran to the Teens.

As soon as Mel saw me, she tried to stab me with the knife.

"Don't hurt me!" I said. "I can help you. A lizard is coming to get you. You must stab it in the neck. That will kill it."

"Thanks," said Carl.

I climbed up the rocks, out of the way.

I looked down and I saw the lizard.

It stood up on two legs and hissed.

Then it ran towards the Teens.

Mel ran behind Carl. She pushed him at
the lizard.

Carl swung the axe but the lizard jumped right
over him.

The lizard grabbed Mel with its claws. She screamed. The lizard opened its huge mouth and bit her.

Mel's screams stopped.

"Kill it while it eats!" I shouted to Carl.

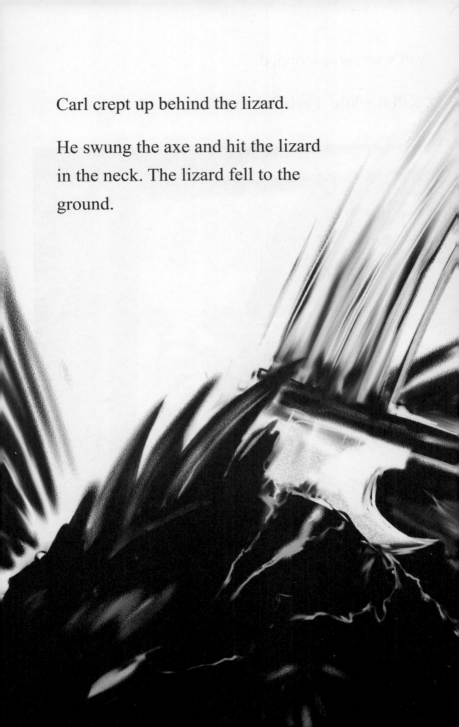

Carl crept up behind the lizard.

He swung the axe and hit the lizard in the neck. The lizard fell to the ground.

The lizard was dead. So was Mel.

"Bye, Mel," said Carl. He walked away.

We heard the Voice.

"Game Over!"